D0294269

TALES FROM Leprechaun LAND

BRENDAN AND THE BLARNEY STONE

STEPHEN WALSH & MARITA O'DONOVAN

Illustrations by Diane Le Feyer

WITHDRAWN FROM STOCK

THE O'BRIEN PRESS

DUBLIN

For

Elenor, Michael, Daniel

About the Authors

Stephen Walsh and Marita O'Donovan are married (to each other). Together, they spend a great deal of time following leprechaun clues in their quest for the gold at the end of the rainbow.

First published 2017 by The O'Brien Press Ltd,
12 Terenure Road East, Rathgar, Dublin 6, D06 HD27, Ireland.
Tel: +353 1 4923333; Fax: +353 1 4922777
E-mail: books@obrien.ie
Website: www.obrien.ie

The O'Brien Press is a member of Publishing Ireland.

Copyright for text © Stephen Walsh and Marita O'Donovan
Copyright for illustration, layout, editing and design © The O'Brien Press Ltd

ISBN: 978-1-84717-723-0

All rights reserved. No part of this book may be
reproduced or utilised in any way or by any means, electronic
or mechanical, including photocopying, recording or by any
information storage and retrieval system without
permission in writing from the publisher.

6 5 4 3 2 1
21 20 19 18 17

Cover and internal illustrations by Diane Le Feyer.
Produced and designed in Ireland. Printed in the EU.
The paper in this book is produced using pulp from managed forests.

Published in:

DUBLIN
UNESCO
City of Literature

Long ago, the leprechauns came to a place where a river gleamed among the rolling hills, and tall trees grew. There, hidden from the human world, on a carpet of shamrocks at the rainbow's end, they made their home and called it Ballynadeenybeg*.

If ever you walk close by, you just might see a wisp of smoke from their turf fires or hear their music whispering in the wind. Search forever but you will never find Ballynadeenybeg – for it is well hidden by the leprechauns, who use their magic to keep it a secret. But look out! The leprechauns may be closer than you think.

* Ballynadeenybeg – from the Irish, meaning 'town of the little people'.

Brendan the leprechaun lived in the village of Ballynadeenybeg. There, he made beautiful musical instruments, and the walls of his little shop were festooned with bodhráns, uilleann pipes, tin whistles, and fiddles and bows.

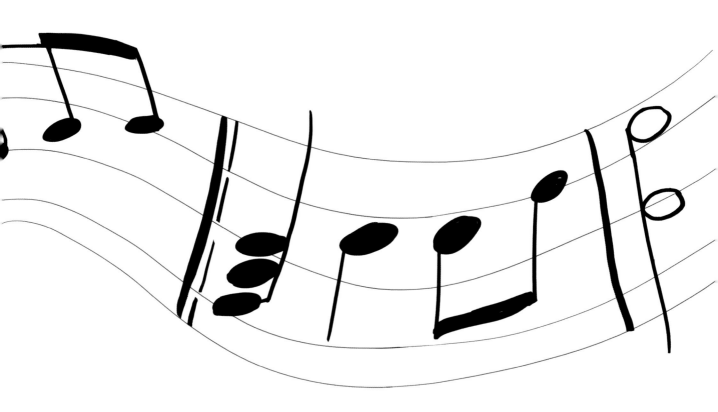

The instruments that Brendan made played music that was sweeter than the sweetest songbird, and leprechauns travelled from the four corners of Ireland to buy his wares, for they knew they were the best in the land.

Brendan himself liked to play the tin whistle, and when he played, everyone stopped to listen. The lilt of his music was so lovely that it touched the very hearts of those who heard it.

However, Brendan had a problem: the moment he opened his mouth to speak, everything went wrong. His words came out in a TERRIBLE jumble and he always said the wrong thing.

This caused Brendan a lot of bother. If he went to buy cheese, he might come home with peas. And once when he went to buy a hat, he came home with a cat. (Fortunately the cat became a beloved pet to Brendan.)

hair
chair
cat hat
whistle
thistle
donkey monkey

pie sky
cheese
peas
plug
slug

PEAS

Every Saturday night, the leprechauns and the fairies gathered for a great céilí, where they danced and sang until daybreak. Brendan and his three friends – Murphy, Mossy and Marty – made up the band.

Murphy played the uilleann pipes, Mossy played the fiddle, and Marty played the bodhrán. Brendan played the tin whistle, of course.

One of those who loved to listen to Brendan play was the beautiful fairy Nuala, who came to the céilí every single Saturday. Brendan was always delighted to see Nuala sitting nearby, tapping her toe in time with the music and smiling towards him.

How he longed to ask Nuala to dance, but he was too afraid to even speak to her for fear of what he might accidentally say.

Brendan went to visit Daire, the oldest leprechaun in Ballynadeenybeg – so old that he knew the answers to most questions.

When Daire heard Brendan's problem, he laughed and said, 'Brendan, you must kiss the Blarney Stone. That will give you the "gift of the gab" and an eloquence beyond your dreams.'

The very next day, Brendan set about making a plan to kiss the famous stone, and Murphy, Mossy and Marty agreed to help him.

And that was how the four leprechaun band members found themselves hiding in a little thicket, watching a group of tourists get out of a bus a mile from Ballynadeenybeg.

(Of course the tourists didn't realise how close they were to the leprechauns' well-hidden home. That would have made their holiday even more special!)

'Who are all these big people?' asked Mossy.

'They are visitors from other lands,' Murphy explained, 'who come to see all the wonderful sights in Ireland.'

While the visitors were off having lunch, the four leprechauns hopped aboard the bus and tucked themselves under a seat, where no one would see them.

Brendan had brought a pocketful of gold coins – a leprechaun never knows when they might come in handy – and Marty had brought some cheese and shamrock sandwiches. 'Please pass the peas and hard-rock sandwiches,' said poor Brendan.

In no time at all, the visitors trooped back onto the bus, and the journey to Blarney began. The leprechauns were very comfortable under the seat, where they had a great view of everyone's shoes.

They could hear the tourists chatting away, admiring the mountains and rivers, the green fields, the farms, the castles and round towers.

Then a lady sitting right above Brendan said, 'I haven't seen a single leprechaun since I came to Ireland.'

The man beside her replied, 'Well, you better keep looking out that window if you want to catch a glimpse of one!'

Brendan, Murphy, Mossy and Marty tried to stifle their laughter. Imagine, the visitors were looking out the window for leprechauns, and four of them were under their seat the whole time!

At last they arrived at the village of Blarney in County Cork. The sun shone, and all the passengers (including four rather small ones) got off the bus. The tourists started lining up to go into the Castle to kiss the Blarney Stone.

Brendan and his friends sat down on a bench and tried to figure out how to get inside without anyone seeing them. There was no obvious entrance for leprechauns.

Then Murphy spotted a tattered old coat thrown over the bench, and it gave him an idea. 'Why don't we stand on each other's shoulders and put this coat over us? Then we can look like one of the big people!'

Leabharlann Contae na Midhe

So Marty stood on Brendan's shoulders, then Mossy stood on Marty's shoulders, and Murphy stood on Mossy's shoulders, and they hoisted the old coat around them.

There was some money in the pocket, which they used to pay the admission fee, and – apart from a few strange looks from the lady selling the tickets – they managed to make it up the steps (more than a hundred of them!) to the top of the Castle.

The leprechauns hid in a corner and watched the tourists kissing the Blarney Stone.

Now, the Stone is set into the battlements at the top of the Castle, and in order to kiss it, you must lie on your back with somebody holding on to you so you don't slip. There are railings just below to stop people falling to the ground, but – oh dear! – a little leprechaun might easily slide through them!

As the last of the visitors were going back down the steps, Murphy had another bright idea. 'Brendan, grab hold of the sleeve of the coat and we'll use it to swing you out to kiss the Stone. We'll swing you three times to make sure you manage it.'

So Murphy, Mossy and Marty
held firmly on to the coat
and swung it out across the
battlements, with Brendan clutching
tightly to the sleeve.

Murphy counted: 'ONE …' (The sleeve
swung out with Brendan hanging on, but his
eyes were shut and he missed the Stone.)

'TWO …' (There was a ripping sound as the stitching
in the coat started to come apart, and Brendan, startled
by the noise, missed again.)

'THREE!' (The ripping sound got louder, but Brendan managed
to stretch out his neck and give the Blarney Stone a great big kiss!)

'Phew!' said Murphy, as they hauled Brendan back to safety. And they all laughed and danced around happily in a big circle.

They grabbed the coat and dragged it down the steps of the Castle, then put it back where they had found it on the bench. They could see all the visitors getting back on the bus for the journey home.

'Come on!' said Mossy. 'We have to run for our bus.'

'Just a minute,' said Brendan, who was busy filling the pockets of the coat with gold coins. 'This old coat was a lucky find for us, so now it will be lucky for someone else!'

On the homeward journey, Murphy, Mossy and Marty had to '*shhhhhh!*' Brendan at least twenty times. The 'gift of the gab' was working, and he was talking nineteen to the dozen, thrilled with his new powers of communication.

The four friends ran home across the fields to Ballynadeenybeg, where it was time for the weekly céilí. The other leprechauns and fairies were overjoyed to see Brendan and his band back again.

After a couple of jigs and reels, Brendan asked Nuala to dance, and she accepted with delight. He told her of his adventures (without mixing up his words), and about how he had kissed the Blarney Stone. Then they danced and danced!

Meanwhile, far away in Blarney, an old man who hadn't had a lucky day for years spied the coat lying on the bench. 'Well, aren't I the lucky one, finding this grand old coat?' he said.

You can imagine how lucky he felt a few seconds later, when he put on the coat and put his hands into the pockets!